The Spirit of the Blue Light

as told by **Marianna Mayer** • illustrations by **Laszlo Gal**

Macmillan Publishing Company / New York • Collier Macmillan Publishers / London

Library of Congress Cataloging-in-Publication Data • Mayer, Marianna. The spirit of the blue light. Summary: A
soldier on his way home from the wars helps out a mysterious old man who rewards him by telling him where to find
the magic blue light. [1. Fairy tales. 2. Folklore — Germany] I. Gal, Laszlo, ill.   II. Title.
PZ8.M4617Sp   1990   398.2'1'0943 [E]   86-12524   ISBN 0-02-765350-1

For Vicki Chatfield Cerruto
— M.M.

To Artolino LaCaprara
for his *vera generosità*
— L.G.

In the kingdom of Sumar, peace was declared. The great war was over, and the king dismissed his troops. Michael, a young foot soldier, had nowhere to go; so he made up his mind to seek adventure in the wide world. After all, he reasoned, a poor lad has very little to lose.

Michael had not journeyed far before he came upon a forest of silver birches. It was springtime, and the bark shimmered white in the sunlight. Villagers living nearby believed the forest was enchanted and told frightful tales about it. But Michael, knowing nothing of such stories, set foot upon the path leading in and did not for a moment look back.

The pale green leaves rustled, and the dark branches sighed as a cool breeze swept through the trees. Michael heard whispering in the bracken, but told himself it was a trick of the wind. Light and shadow shifted along the path with the wavering of the branches. Whispering breezes, patterns of bright silver light moving and changing and moving again — Michael shivered, sensing that the forest was not a place to wander alone.

Suddenly a voice cried out, "Ish! Sticks! Darn things! Ack! Rats!"

Michael hurried toward the cries and found a raggedy man furiously struggling under a great bundle of sticks tied to his back.

"What's your trouble, grandfather? Maybe I can be of help."

"Help? *Help?* I should say so, confound it all! Can't you see, you fool, that this bundle of sticks is too much for me? Give me a hand and be quick about it."

Though Michael was shocked by the old fellow's manner, he responded at once to his distress. Taking up the burden, he shouldered it himself without complaint. Then Michael helped the old man to his feet, and the two stood face-to-face.

"At last! Now, we don't have far to go. But remember, I'm not any-body's *grandfather*. I'll thank you to call me Lawrence, for that's my name. So, come along. I don't have all day to be standing here talking to you." And without another word the raggedy man turned on his heels and walked on.

No sooner had Michael begun to follow than the bundle of sticks grew heavier and heavier until, in fact, he wasn't sure that he could go another step. It crossed his mind to throw off the horrid bundle and be on his way, but he shrugged off the thought and continued to follow Lawrence, who was now far ahead.

By the time they reached the old man's cottage, Michael was exhausted. At last, he dropped to his knees beside the front door and freed himself from the bundle.

Abruptly the man's attitude changed, and he spoke kindly. "It was extremely good of you to help me. When you've rested, I'd like to do something to repay you."

"Oh, there is no need of that," replied Michael.

"On the contrary, I insist. But now you must rest, and when you awake we will have supper."

The old man led Michael to a cot and left him to sleep.

When Michael awoke a few hours later, he felt refreshed and ready to join his host for a bit of supper. They ate before a fire that crackled and sparked with some of the very sticks that Michael had carried. While they watched the flames, Lawrence told a strange tale about a treasure that lay concealed at the center of a great mountain.

"It is called the White Mountain," Lawrence told his companion. "It is here in the forest and, if you search it out, believe me, what lies inside will be beyond anything you've ever imagined."

But Michael was skeptical. "If such a treasure exists, why has it not already been discovered? You yourself might have claimed the riches, instead of telling me about them."

Lawrence pulled slowly at his beard and smiled. "I'm an old man, my boy, and at my age have very little taste for adventure. Besides, it is said that, to enter the White Mountain, one must possess innocence and goodness. You have those qualities. I've seen them in the kindness you have shown me.

"So now I wish to repay you by helping you to seek the great treasure. But you must listen carefully, for this is a magic mountain. In it are three rooms and each holds precious metal: copper, silver, and gold!"

Lawrence leaned closer and whispered, "But there is more: The White Mountain holds a greater secret, for it is the dwelling place of *the blue light*. If you find the blue light, Michael, you shall have everything your heart desires."

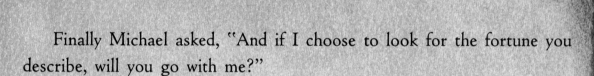

Finally Michael asked, "And if I choose to look for the fortune you describe, will you go with me?"

"Yes, as far as I am able, but I cannot enter the mountain with you. That you must do alone, for he who attempts to enter must possess a pure heart. Few of my advanced age still can claim this—only poets and holy men, of which I am neither. One other sort can enter, as I've already said—kind youths like you, Michael."

"*I?*" exclaimed Michael. "I'm a simple soldier, with not even a king's army to follow any longer."

"It's not might or force that will conquer the guardian of the blue light. Never fear. You have what is needed," Lawrence insisted.

Michael was silent, and the old man went on.

"We will leave before daybreak. Once we've reached the mountain, I shall wait at the tunnel entrance. Then you will go the rest of the way alone. Now rest. I shall wake you just before sunrise."

Michael slept, but only fitfully. His dreams were crowded with shadowy figures looming large about him. Fleeing from their clutches, he entered a pool of pure blue light and stillness. Suddenly, far off in the distance, he heard his name called. Lawrence was standing over him as he opened his eyes.

"Come, it's time. We must be on our way. There is not a moment to lose."

They left the cottage while it was still dark. Silently the two traveled through the forest along an overgrown path. The sun rose slowly, brightening the sky with a soft golden light. As they approached, Michael saw their destination — the mountain — starkly white against the sky. Lawrence urged him on through thorny vines so thick that Michael was forced to hack them with his sword. At last, their efforts were rewarded: Beyond the undergrowth, they found the tunnel into the White Mountain.

"There," whispered Lawrence, as he pushed Michael forward. "Don't be afraid."

Michael turned to look into the old man's eyes, but what he saw made him question all that had gone before, so intent, so fierce did Lawrence look. Perhaps, Michael thought, the old man is mad after all. Michael sighed. Well, I've come this far on a wild errand. I might as well please him and keep on awhile longer. He gave Lawrence a resigned smile, and in he went.

Michael slept, but only fitfully. His dreams were crowded with shadowy figures looming large about him. Fleeing from their clutches, he entered a pool of pure blue light and stillness. Suddenly, far off in the distance, he heard his name called. Lawrence was standing over him as he opened his eyes.

"Come, it's time. We must be on our way. There is not a moment to lose."

They left the cottage while it was still dark. Silently the two traveled through the forest along an overgrown path. The sun rose slowly, brightening the sky with a soft golden light. As they approached, Michael saw their destination — the mountain — starkly white against the sky. Lawrence urged him on through thorny vines so thick that Michael was forced to hack them with his sword. At last, their efforts were rewarded: Beyond the undergrowth, they found the tunnel into the White Mountain.

"There," whispered Lawrence, as he pushed Michael forward. "Don't be afraid."

Michael turned to look into the old man's eyes, but what he saw made him question all that had gone before, so intent, so fierce did Lawrence look. Perhaps, Michael thought, the old man is mad after all. Michael sighed. Well, I've come this far on a wild errand. I might as well please him and keep on awhile longer. He gave Lawrence a resigned smile, and in he went.

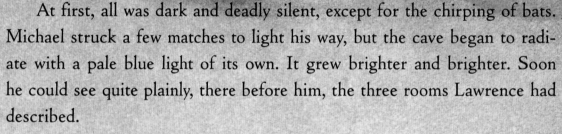

At first, all was dark and deadly silent, except for the chirping of bats. Michael struck a few matches to light his way, but the cave began to radiate with a pale blue light of its own. It grew brighter and brighter. Soon he could see quite plainly, there before him, the three rooms Lawrence had described.

"And so the old fellow was right!" Michael marveled.

He walked slowly into the first room. Copper coins spilled from hundreds of coffers. Too excited to grasp even a handful, he hurried on to the second room, where the brilliance of silver dazzled his eyes. As he hastened into the third room, he was both thrilled and horrified. There was more gold than even a king could wish for! But he heard, at the very same instant, the frightful sound of slow, muffled steps approaching.

A wraithlike figure shrouded in shadows floated toward him and then halted a few feet away. Michael reached for his sword, but doubted it would be any use against such a spirit. They studied each other in silence, neither one moving. Then, slowly, almost imperceptibly, the wraith retreated into the shadows. While Michael watched it fade from sight, the pale blue light grew brighter and brighter.

Only then did the frightened young man see the source of light: a small lantern hanging on a hook at the entrance to the room of gold. Michael grabbed the lantern and ran from the cave, leaving everything — gold, silver, copper — behind.

Once in the daylight, Michael could find no trace of Lawrence. Extinguishing the lantern and tucking it into the folds of his coat, Michael set out in search of him. I will return to the cottage, Michael thought. But the path had disappeared. So he pushed on in what he guessed was the right direction, only to be thwarted at every step. The forest seemed to close in on him, and undergrowth coiled around his feet. He tried to thrash his way through, but lost his footing and stumbled headlong into a covered ditch.

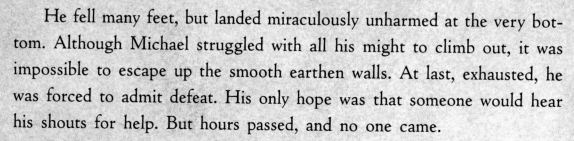

He fell many feet, but landed miraculously unharmed at the very bottom. Although Michael struggled with all his might to climb out, it was impossible to escape up the smooth earthen walls. At last, exhausted, he was forced to admit defeat. His only hope was that someone would hear his shouts for help. But hours passed, and no one came.

As evening set in, Michael remembered the lantern from the cave. When he pulled it from his coat, although he had done nothing to ignite it, blue light immediately flooded the ditch. Raising the lantern high, Michael saw that he was not alone.

"What do you wish of me?" asked the Spirit of the Blue Light.

Michael swallowed hard and said, "Nothing...I —" but stopped speaking when the Spirit raised a shrouded hand to silence him.

"You have brought forth the lamp and summoned me by doing so. What service may I provide you?"

Michael at last began to understand, but it didn't seem possible! Would this phantom actually do his bidding? There was only one way to find out.

"Please," asked Michael, "can you get me out?"

Without a word, the Spirit waved his arms, and in a flash Michael found himself safely out of the ditch. There was no denying what had happened; yet the Spirit had vanished and the light in the lantern was extinguished.

Curious, Michael lighted the lantern once more. Immediately the Spirit reappeared. "I am at your service," he said with a gracious bow.

This time Michael thought carefully as he studied the heavily cloaked stranger. The figure was tall and probably slim, although it was difficult to tell, for the gray cloak reached the ground and the cowled hood remained pulled down so far that the face was completely hidden.

Finally Michael said, "I should like a horse and, perhaps, some money."

The Spirit bowed his head and vanished, but in a moment a horse came walking out of the thicket and stopped just in front of Michael.

If I'm dreaming, thought Michael, may I never wake up. He mounted the horse and set out. Reaching in to place the darkened lantern in his saddlebag, he found there, to his delight, a small purse of gold.

By nightfall Michael rode into a village. At a comfortable inn, he took rooms, deciding to settle at least for a while. One evening not long after his arrival, he stood at his window gazing out into the starry sky. In the distance, high above some small thatched-roof cottages, stood a tower within the walled complex of a royal castle. Michael could just make out, framed in the tower's one lighted window, the slender form of a young woman.

He wondered about that young woman. Night after night he saw her there, and finally he asked the innkeeper who she was.

"That is the king's daughter," the innkeeper told him. "I'm afraid hers is a sad story. Long ago a wizard prophesied that she would marry a common soldier. The king flew into a rage at such a prediction and banished the wizard from the kingdom. Then he shut the princess in the tower. She has been there ever since.

"My young friend, I hope you've no thought to meet her. It would be death to any commoner who tried. The princess is guarded day and night. Forget her, or you will lose your life. Remember, the king knows no mercy where his daughter is concerned."

Michael tried to heed the innkeeper's warning, but he could not forget the princess. At last, simply to be closer to her, he contrived to get work at the royal stables. There he was sometimes able to slip away and stand, for a moment or two, below the tower window high above and steal a glance at her. One day their eyes met. Michael's heart raced with excitement when she gave him the hint of a smile before retreating from the window.

Afterward it was as though Michael were bewitched. Indeed, the princess was all he could think about. He became obsessed with finding a way to meet her. By day he worked at the castle, hoping for another chance to see her, and at night he spent countless hours at the window in his room watching for her.

At last, one moonless night, Michael lighted his lantern. The room glowed with blue light, and the Spirit appeared.

"What do you wish?"

"I wish to meet the princess who is kept in the tower," said Michael.

Instantly the Spirit was gone but soon reappeared with the princess. Michael bowed low in respect, like the noble young soldier he was, and the princess extended her hand for him to rise.

"You are the young man who works at the stables, are you not? I have dreamed of you before. What is your name?" asked the princess.

Michael told her his name but was so struck by the miracle of their meeting that he could not say more at first. Shy and awkward, the two managed in a short time to feel comfortable with each other and even to laugh easily together. But the princess thought that she was still dreaming, and Michael was too afraid of frightening her to tell her otherwise. After a little time passed, the Spirit stepped forward to take the princess back to the tower. Her smile was sad, for she was sorry to go; and, as Michael saw them vanish, he vowed one day to rescue the princess and make her his wife.

But some things are easier to wish than to do, as Michael was soon to learn. The next day the princess recounted her dream to her father. When the king heard of the young and handsome soldier, he was very much disturbed. That evening he issued orders to double the guards that surrounded the tower. Then he summoned an aged maidservant to his private chamber.

"From now on you will remain by the princess's side both day and night," the king told the maid. "Under no circumstance will you leave her, without my permission. A bed for you will be placed in her room. Remember, it will be most unfortunate for you if the princess escapes your watchfulness."

Encouraged by his successful meeting with the princess, Michael sent the Spirit to fetch her again that night. Everything went as expected, for the maidservant feigned sleep when the Spirit appeared. But when he left with the princess, the maid jumped up from her bed and followed. A skill-

ful spy, she found the inn; but, lacking real courage, she did not enter. Instead, she marked the door with chalk so that, later, the king's guards would be able to pick it out from the others.

The following day the king sent guards to find the marked door, but the Spirit had marked every door in the village. Learning of the clever trick that had spoiled his plan, the king grew very angry.

In secret he warned the maid, "You have failed me once. I shall have your life if you fail again. Now, then, take this pouch of gold dust and fasten it to the princess's nightdress. Make sure that not even my daughter knows what you have done. A small hole in one corner of the pouch will leak a trickle of gold and leave a trail for me to follow. If you don't succeed, old woman, I will show you no mercy."

The maidservant trembled as she carried out the king's order. Then, her task complete, she crept into the shadows and waited. At nightfall, the Spirit came for the princess, and this time he was none the wiser.

It was an easy task for the guards to follow the trail of gleaming gold dust in the sunlight the following day. Surrounding the inn, they burst in and captured poor Michael, placed him in irons, and marched him before the king. Though he had done nothing wicked, Michael was condemned to be hanged.

Alone in his cell, Michael was in despair, for he had forgotten the lantern when the guards surprised him. On the morning he was to be hanged, his friend the innkeeper was allowed to visit.

"My dear Michael, I'm afraid there is no hope of saving you," said the innkeeper. "Although the people are in an uproar, the king will hear none of it. Even the princess has pleaded for your life, but her tears have seemed only to make the king more convinced that you must die. I think he fears you have stolen her heart and for this reason will show you no mercy."

"Don't waste your pity on me, friend," said Michael. "You warned me of the king's wrath. But I would risk all again in the hope of seeing the princess. If she loves me, as you say, then I will find the courage to face what I must. Now, if you will, let me ask one last favor. Bring me the small bundle that I left in my room. Tell the guards that I wish to divide my few belongings among my friends. But please go quickly. There is not much time."

The innkeeper was happy to oblige and quickly returned with the bundle. As soon as he was alone, Michael drew out the lantern and summoned the Spirit.

"Although the king has commanded you to die," the Spirit said, "I will not forsake you. Ask to light your pipe for one final smoke just before you are to be hanged. The king won't deny you this. Conceal the lantern beneath your jacket, and use the flame to light your pipe."

Just then Michael heard steps approaching, and the Spirit vanished.

The guards took him to the gallows. The hour of his execution was at hand. He faced the king and asked for one last smoke from his pipe.

"This I will permit," said the king.

Michael took out the lantern, lighted his pipe from its blue flame, and the Spirit rose up in all his awesome grandeur.

"What do you command?" he asked the condemned soldier.

"Capture those enemies who have wished me harm."

The Spirit of the Blue Light grew enormous. Brandishing a mighty sword, he descended on the king and the horrified guards, striking in every direction. His cloak flew in the wind as he swooped down upon them, seeming to be everywhere at once. His fury terrified the guards, and they begged for mercy as they dropped their weapons.

Finally, amidst the cheering crowd, the king fell to his knees and humbly called out to Michael for pity.

"I will spare you, if you allow the princess to marry me."

"You have my permission and half my kingdom. Only call off your henchman," pleaded the beaten king.

Turning to the Spirit who had served him so loyally, Michael said, "I give the power of the blue light back to you." And with that, he handed the lantern to the Spirit.

As the Spirit accepted, he pushed back his hood, revealing his face. The king gave a gasp of recognition, for here was the very wizard he had banished. But Michael recognized him at once as Lawrence and embraced his friend. The princess stepped forward to thank the wise man who had helped make the prophecy come true. The people rejoiced, for the wizard had always been a great favorite among them.

That very day a lavish celebration took place, and the king married his daughter to the fine young soldier. As a wedding gift, as he had promised, the king gave them half the kingdom. Michael and the princess lived the rest of their days in peace and contentment and, after the old king's death, ruled wisely and justly throughout the land.